It's Complicated

Flairs and Glairs

Publication House

"It's Complicated"

ISBN No: 978-93-90799-66-4
1st Edition
Language – English and Hindi

Flairs and Glairs
Publication House
Regd. Under MSME Act.

Disclaimer

This is a work of fiction and solely represent the thoughts of the corresponding authors of the articles. Our editors have tried their best to edit the content of all the authors and check the plagiarism.

All the write-ups in this book are unique and are only published in this book.

In case any plagiarism or error is found, only the author is responsible alone, and not the publisher or the Compilers.

Cover Designing and Book Formatting
Shubham Shah and Ishani Agarwal

Co Author

Shubham Shah (Founder Flairs and Glairs)
Ishani Agarwal (Co-Founder Flairs and Glairs)
Sachin Banoudhiya(Compiler)

1. 1.Pragya Verma
2. 2.Darshan Patel
3. 3.Miral Dhokiya
4. Reetika Singh
5. Punita Sinha
6. Vedika Agarwal
7. Suggala Keerthi Sai Sharanya
8. Bathula Veekshitha
9. Christy Gnana Deepa. J
10. Vaishnavi Hend
11. Moina
12. 12.Sahina Ghugha
13. Neena Taimoori
14. Arshi Fatima
15. Muskan Sahu
16. Sumedha Walia
17. 17.Rashmika Aitha
18. Kalamkaar
19. 19.Laxmi Mondal
20. 20.. Srijani Das
21. Yatri Patel
22. Niva Patra
23. Ms. Ishrat Jahan Noormohammed Khan
24. Sanjay Naik
25. Sanoj Kumar
26. Jaya Bhardwaj

27. Roohi Prasad
28. Neha Raghav
29. 29.Ipsita Panigrahi
30. Pankaj Sharma
31. Divyanshi Goel
32. Diksha Motwani
33. Kiruthika C
34. Priyanka Sharma
35. Chandni Kesharwani
36. Gautam Saini
37. Nagma Tarannum
38. Adarsh Singh
39. Jaya Chandana
40. Pooja Desai
41. Soundarya Mohan
42. Manas Pradhan
43. Sakshi Sharma
44. Debesh Prusty
45. Gautam Kushwah
46. Vaibhava Suri
47. Krishna Motwani
48. Jayashree Sahoo
49. Pratham Mittal
50. 50.Arju Mali

Shubham Shah

(Founder- Flairs and Glairs)

Shubham Shah, an entrepreneur at "Flairs & Glairs" a brand with dynamics in events organizing and cultural educational pan INDIA, is a 26yrs old guy who recently has entered the digital platform of imprinting emotions. He has initiated with his own open mic platform to help budding poets and aspiring writers under his brand named as "Teekhe Zasbaaat"

He is a commerce graduate from the Bhagalpur City of Bihar.

He states Writing has impersonated him since childhood and he has now been writing for over a decade!

Cooking, on the other hand, is his passion! He also mentions, trying out new things just tickles him!

When asked sir, Why SPICY EMOTIONS?

He smiled and added, "agar jasbaat teekhe na ho toh wo jasbaat kahan" Spices are all that blends! So do his words!

As a chef, he presents to you his dish! Hot and freshly served! Taste it! Feel it! Enjoy it! You can also find his writing in the Book "Teekhe Zasbaaat" and 50+ Co-authored anthologies. With his passion to explore opportunities across Platforms, he is working with keen devotion and We wish him all the very best for his future ventures.

He is Featured in the **International Magazine De-Mode** for his upcoming solo novel.

He is **Approved by Ne8x for its Lit Fest,** and is a **Golden Star Awards 2020 Winner.**

He is an **India Book of Records Holder** for his Anthology **Satrang,** and has the **Grandmaster** title by **Asia Book of Records**, for the same.

He has also been featured in **Prabhat Khabar, Dainik Jagran** and other renowned Newspaper for his achievements. He has also been awarded with **India Star Republic Award 2021.**

He has been a proud co-author to

India Book of Records (Title- Black)

World Book of Records (Title -15 Wonders of Poetries)

India Book of Records (Title - Aaina)

Vajra World Records Holder (Title - Gustakhi Maaf Hai)

High Range of Records Holder (Title - Gustakhi Maaf Hai)

Share your reviews on his

@spicy_emotions
@shubham4shah

Or via email on

shubham2shah@gmail.com

To stay tuned to his work and opportunities follow his business Handles

INSTAGRAM   FACEBOOK   YOUTUBE

@flairsandglairs
@teekhezasbaaat

WEBSITE:

https://flairsandglairs.in/
https://flairsandglairs.com/

Ishani Agarwal

(Co-Founder- Flairs and Glairs)

Ishani Agarwal hails from the City of Joy, Kolkata.
She is the co-founder of her Community "Teekhe Zasbaaat"
and Flairs and Glairs Publication.
Been a Compiler for 45+ Anthologies, she is in the process
for more. Co-authored in 150+ Anthologies. She is a India
Book of Records Holder, a Vajra World Records Holder, a
High Range of Records Holder and a Bravo Record holder.

Approved by Ne8x for its Lit Fest 2020, and Literary Icon 2020. Also a Golden Star Awards Winner 2020.

She has also been awarded with India Star Republic Award 2021.

She has been featured by the National Magazine "Taree Zameen Par" with the title 'unstoppable'.

Also featured in the International Magazine DeMode for her upcoming solo novel, she is proud to write on social issues, and is happy with the love she is receiving.

Connect with her on Instagram: @Ishani_agarwal_quotes / @compilations_so_far

Sachin Banoudhiya (Compiler)

Sachin Banoudhiya is an aspiring 21 year old Poet and author. He is a published author in 50+ anthologies and compiler of 2 ongoing anthologies . He is A Student of Bsc. He is currently the permanent staff serving his duties in the Global Hospital, His dreams are extreme and he also has the passion to fulfill them.

 You can get him by search His name On Google.

Instagram - Sachin_banoudhiya

Gmail - sachinbanoudhiya@gmail.com

YouTube- Writeups from Sachin

इजहार-ए-मोहब्बत

काफी कुछ बातें है
जो मुझे तुमसे करनी है,
दिल से दिल की मुलाकातें है
जो मुझे तुमसे मिलकर करनी है,

अपनी बातों से इस भटके दिल को
प्यार सा सुकून का ठहराव दोगी?
मेरे दिल की इन कश्मकश का
मेरे दिल को रिझाने लायक जवाब दोगी

धड़कते दिल की उस धड़कन को
अपने मीठे सुरों का पैग़ाम दोगी?

उन अंगड़ाई में लिपटी सुबह की दस्तक
अपनी नाम आंखो से भीगी शामों में सिमट
हर पल को अपने मेरे साथ बिताना चाहोगी ?

मिलों एक बार तुमसे
बात-ए-दिल बयां करनी है,
दिल से दिल की मुलाकातें है
जो मुझे तुमसे मिल कर करनी है!!!

It's Complicated

I meet you every day in my thoughts,
 but in reality there is distance of miles we've,
The feeling and smile on my face while imagining you those
can't be hidden ,

The day I saw you for the first time, this desire came out of
my heart, is there anything more beautiful than this ?
It is not possible for us to be one, but as long as I am alive I
will live every moment for you

Look at you and smile at me, look at me like this, I feel like
you love me too as I do
But I KNOW That's just my imagination
Yes I know IT'S COMPLICATED .

Pragya Verma

Pragya Verma hails from Prayagraj, Uttar Pradesh. She is a poetess and a writer. She has done 75+ anthologies, and two international anthologies and currently doing two world record anthologies as a co-author. She is also compiling her own anthology named, "SHADES OF NIGHT". She has a great interest in making paintings and doing photography. She loves to gain spiritual knowledge and tries to find peace everywhere. You can follow her on Instagram: @wordsofpragya

Mine Forever

He has a love in his eyes,
In which, all my happiness lies.
With him there's no scary nights,
Every moment feels delight.

He is as calm as river,
With whom I can live forever.
His smile is like a rainbow,
That takes away my sorrow.

The peace I get with him,
That couldn't be found at the rim.
Nightmares don't scare me now,
As he stays with me anyhow.

I feel calmness of river in his love,
His love makes me shine brighter than the stars above.
He brought light in my dark life,
From my heart, he had removed all the strife.

I want his love forever and ever,
Oh lord, just make this man mine forever.

Shower of your Love

The shower of your love,
The safety in your arms,
All these things are all of the above.
Your memories bring all of your charms.

Your pure heart, your true care,
You are someone i don't want to lose I swear.
Sweet, bitter, crazy memories with you,
Is something that will keep me always close to you.

No lies, no cries,
I only want to see your laughter and smiles.
I hate that time when you are not around,
You healed me and recovered my wound.

The day i found you I will never forget,
I want you to me mine in every life i get

Darshan Patel

Here by Darshan Patel physiotherapist, co author who writes about life and with the aim to inspire a one and motivate to those who loose their hope in life and also about that fact of life. A true inspiration from chaanakya niti, bhagwat geeta, santram saurabh, social media, and learning lessons from ones life.

I LOVE YOU

I love you, it doesn't means, I love your beauty but,
I love your feelings, your character your nature!
I love you, it doesn't means, I love your currency but,
I love your knowledge, which you served me.
I love lot many things in the world, it doesn't means,
I hate you!
You are unforgettable one in my life.
If I doubt you, it doesn't mean,
I love you!
Love is a thing which should not have doubt,
It is not that we can only love our opposite sex,
But we can love each and everyone!
Although anger has more power but,
Not much more than love,
Love has power to change the world!
And upcoming future of man.

Love is a cursory

Love is a cursory of beauty!
It's the heartbeats of two hearts!
That brings together the minds of naughty,
Love is life living lashing process of art.

Love enhance the beauty of man!
To sketch the lining in our hands is the ability of love.
Love makes his lover of her fan.
To become Blind loss of control is the disorder of love.

Mallow gestures makes Mammon.
Mountaineering step by step of our life.
Manageress Mind of Man in common.
Mortuary mosaic in absence of you!

Miral Dhokiya

she is 23 years old trying to turn her words in various ways like shayaris, poetries , quotes etc. there is her first anthology as co-author.

<u>मोहब्बत करने से आसान मरना है ..</u>

मुझे कोई ऐसे आशिक से मिलाओ
जो मोहब्बत में रोया ना हो ।
जो मोहब्बत में हारा ना हो ।
जिसे मोहब्बत में गम ना मिला हो
जिसे मोहब्बत में धोखा ना मिला हो
जिसे मोहब्बत में आंसू ना मिले हो
कभी पूछना उस सच्चे आशिक से बताएगा तुम्हें मोहब्बत करने
से आसान मरना है ।

इस मतलबी दुनिया में कोई अपना ढूंढ रहा हूं जिंदगी भर साथ दे
ऐसा साथी ढूंढ रहा हूं वादे तो कई किए कितनों ने पर जो निभाए
ऐसा हमसफर ढूंढ रहा हूं

आखिर मोहबत करना आसान कहाँ..

उसके बगेर कहीं और दिल लगाना आसान कहाँ..

उसकी याद आज भी आती
पर उसके साथ रहना अब मुमकिन कहाँ..

जुदा तो हो गए वो ये कहकर की अब हमे तुमसे मोहाबत नहीं
पर आज भी उसके इंतजार में खडी हूं मैं
की सायद वो आकर कहदे की तुम्हारे बगर हमारा भी कहीं ओर
दिल लगाना आसान कहाँ..

आखिर मोहबत करना आसान कहाँ..

Reetika Singh

This is Reetika Singh. Born in Mokama, Bihar in 2001. She is 19 and currently pursuing B.com Honours with CMA USA at Graphic Era Deemed to be University. She has completed her diploma in Karate Shotokan 1st Dan. She has a versatile nature and calm mind. Besides writing she is an virtual artist also.

Rishte

Rishte hawa ki tarah hone chaiye
Khamosh magar aas paas.

Nigah

Khariyiat nahi puchta magar meri khabar rakhta hai,
Maine suna hai woh mujh par nazar rakhta hai.

Punita Sinha

Punita Sinha considers herself a learner and an observer and her first love to be music and words . She isn't good at telling out loud her feelings therefore,she writes . She's someone who can travel miles alone only if she's earphones on ,a camera of any sort to capture and something to write upon.

STAY

I asked you to stay but you easily left,
Didn't you know the love my heart hold for you?
I ask you why,why ,why you thought
Leaving was hard than staying?

I loved you more than I thought I could and
I cared for you more than some of my relatives;
How were you so reckless to not see my love?
I cried thousand nights thinking that you'll return,
Only waking up to more news of the heartful loss,
Knowing that you won't ever be back again!

Now I've this hole in my heart
And I don't know it ever will be filled,
But I know this much that I lost a part of me
And my heart still weeps for a closure is now,
A closure is all what I now need !!

Would You!

Seeing the cutest movie
My head spins
Are you anywhere in my life
Or somewhere far playing in the fields

Would you bring butterflies in my stomach
And left me in awe
Would you make me feel that I'm most pretty
And we're just wow
Would you kiss me in front of everyone
And let everyone know we're one
Would you hold me tight
And be my love even when our hairs are white
Would you fight with others just for me
And make time for me even when you're not free
Would you bring me chocolates and gifts
And let other people know we're lit
Would you understand me like I have never been
And keep me from sinking even if I've been mean
Would you hold on to me even if I try to go
And let others know what it's actually meant by "forever to go"
Would you always stop my cries
And always be my side
Would it all ever happen
And this girl would feel that heaven
Or Would all of it would just be a lie
And this girl would never see such a pure tie

Vedika Agarwal

She is Vedika Agarwal a student of Bsc home science, Delhi university. She likes to write and draw a sketch. She is passionate for dancing, singing and acting. She is a determined, bold and a kind hearted girl. She is very conducive in nature. She loves to spend her leisure with old age home people and orphanage children. She loves to learn new things. She is a very emotional girl. She loves to help others. She loves to write. She has a very helpful and loving nature towards the people.

Long Distance Relationships

Relationship is something with whom we are comfortable can share everything, a person who is always there with us in our good and bad times.

Relationships like long distance are always a great burden, but with Love and Passion, they can be wonderful and true like a real relationship! ...

Many problems hit every relationship, it doesn't matter if it is a normal or an long distance relationship. But there are some special problems that occur in long distance relationships, that don't appear in normal ones, for example it is a big problem, that you cant always physically see each other being so far away. And never be able to hug or spend time with each other in reality so sometimes it can be so depressing, that the relationship might breaks.But nonetheless, if a bond is strong enough, and the couple can see each other from time to time, its guaranteed that the relationship can be strong and withstanding! Many couples see their perspective of being one day to be together, and that's always a big help for saving one's relationship. Not having that chance often destroys it too, because for most couples its not a perspective worth fighting for it!

Of course, there is also a huge chance of cheating, many people in a long distance relationship start to find other partners and its natural and more appealing to have a real, physical person near you, that's also a great risk such a Kind of relationship has in it!

But nonetheless, with much willpower, true Love, Passion and Perspective both partners want to look forward, such a relationship can be beautiful and have a great experience. Nowadays, many relationships like that are existing, many of them work and create couples, that last happy for many years. So there is complications in everything we do but it depends on us how we deal with it either in a positive manner or in a negative manner. A true love never ends and it doesn't matter that it's long distance or like the normal one where we can met. So how long the distance between two people that doesn't matter the love, respect, understanding and care matters the most. In the end I just want to say nothing is complicated just try handling the things which can make it being normal and to live happily.

Suggala Keerthi sai sharanya

She is a student of BBA final year and she is from a small village but having big dreams. She is interested in writing from 6th class and started to write on different social media platforms. She works hard for anything she dreams of and also she is a strong, active, happy girl. She wants become a HR manager and a successful writer and a film maker too and she is working on it to achieve all her dreams

Precious Eternal love

Life is what being loved and every love we face in our life's is very precious because when we really love something we don't want to lose it by any chance. Now I will share a story of a girl who had an complicated love life. There is a girl called "seetha" she was in love with a guy called "raghu". They were in a relation from past 3 years and they had an amazing love life together shared so much happiness, sadness, struggles and many memories too but unfortunately there is a huge mis understanding between them and that made them broke from the relation. Raghu was extremely happy to leave seetha Because he wanted to broke this relationship from past 1 year and unfortunately that happened. Seetha was very depressed and being sad and she felt very low in her life, she even cried for hours Because of her helpless situation.

After bearing all the pain for 4 months suddenly she met a guy called "ram" in facebook from the same town she was living in and there are some mutual friends for them too so she accepted his request and started talking to him and she was relieving from the pain she had before. Days passed one day unfortunately ram and Seetha met at a place and that meeting changed the whole impressions on each other. They started liking each other but she felt bad for being loved and liking him because she had a very bad past but she shared everything with him and he accepted it. As they both stay at same town they continuosly met for lunch and they spent good time together and their like started becoming love. They both never expressed it but they knew that they are loving eachother. They both liked their company. They both were happy together and enjoyed every moment happily. He made her meet all his friends and family just to make her happy and relive from the phase she is. And the same way his

family and friends all accepted her because she is so childish and very talkative and a very good dignified girl with so much maturity and much more understanding abilities she had. One fine day he expressed his love to her and you all know what will be the answer and it was an very happy ending to the complicated relationship she had with her ex boyfriend and felt bad to accept the new one in her life. But finally "SHE SAID YES".

Bathula Veekshitha

She is a young poetess named Veekshitha from Telangana, India. She is the daughter of Late - Veeraiah and Annapurna. The themes of her writings are focused on emotional issues with an emotional touch. Besides being a poetess she is an artist, painter and script writer. She also worked in 'The Uncertain period' anthology book. She has been felicitated by Nipuna and Prathibha awards for her excellence in education. She owe all her success and motivation to all her readers.she is just a beginner with billions of thoughts in her heart...

Eternal Love

She smiled when I was happy
She cried when I was sad

She always taught me a good manners
She was the reason behind my photo in banners

She sacrificed her meal to fill my stomach
She sacrificed her sleep to cure my illness

She taught me how to walk
She taught me how to talk

She made me her world
She made me her life

Oh my dear,

There is no other love greater than mother's
There is no other mother greater than mine...

Ask my heart

Ask my heart,
How many sleepless nights it spent with tears
Ask my heart,
How many nightmares of seeing you with someone else went
with fears

Ask my heart,
How fast it beats when our memories flashes
Ask my heart ,
How hard it feels by remembering our clashes

Ask my heart,
How depressed it was with a different smile
Ask my heart,
How depressed it was to live for a while

Oh my dear,

Ask my heart,
How it always says right though it stays left
Ask my heart,
How it still works when you promised to never leave and left

Christy Gnana Deepa. J

Christy Gnana Deepa , writer pursuing her Undergraduate in English literature in Madurai, Tamilnadu, India. She is a compiler of two anthologies, SECLUDED HEARTS and THE ARDENT HEARTS. Moreover, she is a co-author of more than 25 Anthologies. A writer by passion and a literarian by profession. You can follow her for more writeups in Instagram as ___budding___writer

LOVE DREAM

I Smiled at you every second,
I Missed you every Minute,
I Kissed you every hour,
I Hugged you every day,
I laid you in my arms every week,
I Met you every month,
I spent with you every year..,
But, When I woke up
I found everything was just a Dream!!!

BRUISE

The time we get battered is only
When our loved ones cheat us..!!!

1. In life you have nothing
When you miss your something
Who was your everything!!

2. Love yourself to analyse more about you. You are the
lover of youself.

3. Alphabets love:

I'm the lover of letters. Letters transform me, Pour your
emotions to letters to transform yourself.

Vaishnavi Hend

Vaishnavi Hend lives in the orange city- Nagpur. She is conceptual and curious to create herself. She loves to create, communicate and share her thoughts with her poetry and writings. She is a creator by habit, a microbiologist by occupation and an amateur writer by her own choice. You can get to her by typing Blink2Think-B2T on YouTube.

Evolution of Love

"LOVE"- the strong emotional feeling of affection. When you feel it, your heart starts pumping more oxygen and beats faster than ever, your body starts secreting a number of hormones which excites you. Various streams explains this term as stated by them, a biologist will relate it with reproduction process, relation of love with the reactions occurring in our body will be explained in chemistry , a psychologist will relate it with the theory of attachment and acceptance and so on. Love has its own different definitions and explanations in every region, every language, everywhere, but the understanding, the sightedness regarding love is changing with changing time. Love is the thing which we didn't invent, it was simply discovered."Discovered by us, within ourselves".

But in this modern materialistic era, love is somewhat or somehow disappearing within ourselves. Earlier this pure feeling has the purity, meaning, worth and purpose. But today, the journey of love begins with lust. People these days don't understand the divinity of love. What they are doing is not called love but unfortunately they are calling it love! I have heard a pure love story of an old lady and her husband- "How he bought her the white ambrosial flowers every single day without any fail, how she was always humming his favorite song while cooking for him, how she teases him by doing annoying things, how they always used to fight on small things and shout on each other but, he always held her hand while walking with her. How they always share their love in little things."

And this story made me realise, how love is a beautiful ongoing process which improves day by day. In olden time, the intensity of love was so high that it leads to the growth of those individuals who were in love. Nowadays people are

falling in love, but earlier they were rising in love, growing with each other's strengths and weaknesses. Evolution is the process of change and development. Each and every thing around us, within us has passed from the process of "Evolution". Evolution bring transformation- which is necessary for us.

But evolution of thoughts, evolution of love is erroneous.

I have read about the word "Lagom" in an article, which is a Swedish word meaning not too much, not too little, but just the right amount. Love is becoming Lust these days, too much love spoils people and too little spoils their bond. We need to understand the real meaning of love, we need to reinforce the real feeling of love within us. We always studied about the evolution of our surrounding, our earth, but now we need to understand the real meaning of evolution of our thoughts, and also the "Evolution of Love".

"The four letter word Love should not get Evolved to become a four letter word Lust.

But, the four letter word Love should get Evolved to become a five letter word Lagom "

Moina(Malabika D)

Moina(a.k.a Malabika) is a fellow student, currently living in guwahati Assam. Likes to read, write and travel

लफ्ज़-ए-मोहब्बत

खामियां थी मुझमें, पता था मुझे..
गिन जो तू भी रहा था इसकी खबर ना थी...

इस ऊषा के नज़ारे हसीन,
पिंदार-ए-मोहब्बत भी दिखाता हैं...।

किसी ज़माने से थी जमी धूल
इस दूकान-ए-दिल में,
तेरी कदमों की आहट भर से ही चमकने लगी..।

शब-ए-ग़म में हूं डूबा इस कदर,
अब तो हर रंग फीका सा लगता हैं..।

कैसे बयां करू लफ्ज़-ए-मोहब्बत,
ये तो बस हलक तक आकर रूठ जाती हैं..।

ख़ुश रहता था बहुत मैं जब तक तूने दरकिनार ना कर दिया था।

एक सबब हैं उसकी हर नज़ाकत में
यूहीं नहीं सुब्ह-ओ-शाम-ए-दिल धड़कता..।

उसने ऐसा कहर ढाया हैं मुझमें,
मकतब-ए-इश्क़ में तक पीछे छूटता जा रहा हूं..।

Sahina Ghugha

Sahina Ghugha is 20 year old b.com student at Saurashtra university Rajkot. She is from Jamnagar city of Gujarat. She is state level winner in poetry competition 2017. She is Co-author of 10+ anthologies. She is an amazing writer and poet and she wants do something for society through her pen.

Insta ID:-
Itz_Sahina_write

फनाह

इश्क़ तेरे में, मैं फनाह हो जाऊं
तेरी चाहत में कुछ ऐसे मैं तबाह हो जाऊं
ना जानूं मैं दुनियादारी, हो जाऊं इनसे परे
तुझ ही को अपना मान, तेरी पनाह में सो जाऊं।

तू मेरी ज़िन्दगी की एक कहानी, तू किस्सा है
तू मेरी रूह, मेरी रागिनी का हिस्सा है
तू मेरा वजूद, तुझमें बसी दुआए मेरी
तू मेरी सांसे है, तुझ से बहेती फिजाएं कहीं

मैं हूं कोई चंदा, तू हो इसकी चांदनी कोई
हूं अगर मैं राग जो, तुझ में बसती रागिनी मेरी
खो जाऊं में जिस जहां में, तू वैसा कोई ख्वाब है
अच्छाई बस तुझ में है दिखती, बाकी सब खराब है

आंसू की मनमानी

रो देती हूं मुस्कुरा कर भी,
मगर वो आंसू खुशी के नहीं होते।
दर्द बहुत छुपाए है दिल में,
आंखो में अब उम्मीदों के बादल नहीं होते।
बादल जब भी भारी हो जाए,
तो बरसात की कहानी बन जाए।
दिल में दर्द ज्यादा जम जाए,
तो आंसू की मनमानी हो जाए।

आंखो में नहीं दिखते आंसू,
पर भीतर का सैलाब बहा दे।
ये वो चिंगारी है आंखो की,
जो पानी को तेज़ाब बना दे।
रातों को बहाकर सुकून मिल जाता है,
कुछ तकीये की भी महेरबानी हो जाए।
दिल में दर्द ज्यादा जम जाए,
तो आंसू की मनमानी हो जाए।

Neena Taimoori

Neena is an emerging poet and writer trying to reach beyond the skies of literary and philosophical feasts. She has completed her intermediate, loves art and craft. Celebrates penning down poesy and fancies of her own.
Her integrity endeavour bestow her wings to fly!

Ehsaas

Takleef mn tmhn dekh,
sarh'ana chahti hu.
Muskurate huae dekh,
aur beja hasana chahti hu.
Ansu jo tmhary behne lge,
un ansu'on ko ma churana chahti hu.
Jante nh ho tm kia rkhte ho ehmiyat,
yehi to ehsas tm mn jagana chahti hu.
Du'aen yehi krti hu apne Rab se,
anch tm pr kbhe na aye!
Khusshiyan sab tmhare, qadmon mein sim'tein rhen,
bin mangy tmhn sb kch yun miljae!

I Cherish Me

I honour myself, as I adore how flawed I am.
I exist as a showcase of, contradictory elements.

I struggle for eternity, else I procrastinate.
I devour excessively or famish myself to death.

I trust His species if not, I dislike everyone alive.
I deliver my all or nothing at any price.

This is me and I breathe nay ashamed of aught.
I believe what I am, thwarts to what ye can't subsist!

Arshi Fatima

Arshi Fatima, 18 y/o. She lives in Meerut, She like to read fiction novels, Her dream is to be a successful author, a storyteller, and a good human being. She like sketching, K-pop, and of-course writing. She is currently working on her first novel. She is also a blogger on mirakee, and her ig- the_insane_words17, She is also a Co-author in many anthologies. Her main aim is to inspire others and make them feel that they are not alone. You can also contact her through Email - writeraaru17@gmail.com

Peace In You

I found peace in you,
I found home in you.
I found my happiness in you,
A little pain, a little silence, a lot more love in you.

I found love in you,
I found strength in your presence!
But sadly,
I feel so low in your absence!

I found peace in you..
Oh!
I found my home in your arms.
I found love in your care..
Oh!
I found peace in you.
In this fake world,
I've finally found something real in you.
Oh!

I found peace in you,
I found home in you.
I found my happiness in you.
A little pain, a little silence,
and yes, a lot more love in you.

My Knight

Every night,
I'd fight with the demons.
The demons I carry,
inside my wounded heart.

Every night,
I try to hurt myself.
Every night,
I start crying for no reason!

But, since I met you,
My love!
Your love had made those demons vanish away,
your love had made my wounded heart proceed healing.

To be honest,
You're my Saviour!
You brought me victory,
your love is my victory!

You healed me,
you healed my damaged heart.
You've brought me back to life,
you're my sunshine.
My knight in shining armour!

Muskan sahu

Hello there !!
She is Muskan sahu,a name with smiles and colourful dreams. Obsessed for her writeups. She is currently a student.Her hometown is raipur chhattisgarh. She is an optimistic late night paper scribbler. Her thoughts are justified to the people world around .she is a shayar and writes poetries too. She is passionate about dancing traveling and photography too.

"KOI TOH HO

Koi toh ho jo dekhe toh dekhe sirf mjhe,
Hath tham gale se lagaye or kbhi dur na jaaye...
Rishta koi bhi ho, fark ye nhi..
Bss baat itni h samjh jaaye wo maheez meri baato se,
Mera hasna rona sab sambhal le wo ,
Alfaazo pe nahi, jazbaato ko mahsus kare ...
Tuti hai divaare dil ke har kone ki ,
Jo karde unki marammat aysa koi toh ho...
Jo samjhe uss muskuraahat ke peeche ki sachai ...
Jo khehde tum muskura toh rahi ho magar dil se nahi, kya
baat h jo bata de...
Koi toh ho jo aaye aur bss rehnuma ban jaaye ,
Kaya ko bhul sirf rooh se apna ban jaaye...
Koi toh ho jiski maujudgi shabo-shaam ban jaaye...
Khair, yeh mahaaz alfaaz hi hai, inhe muqammal koi kar na
paaye ....
Aysa koi toh ho jo inn sawaalo ki raazi ban jaaye !!

Ankahe jazbaat

Pyar ishq mohabbat mahaz alfaaz hi reh gye na,
Aakhir chodh toh tum akele hi gye....
Jaan kheh kar kuch yuh anjaan bana gaye...
Tareffe krte hue dusro ki hi aache lgte the, dukh mujhe lage
toh kuch shabd mere naam kr diya krte the....
Tabbajo humse se zyda toh kisi aur ke liye thi, chahe atit ho
ya bhavisy thi ,
Yaade toh khair hum bhulne ki koshish bhi kar jaye, magar
unn ehsaaso ka kya,
Kbhi uss do pal ki muskan ke liy muskuraate the toh kbhi uss
khushi ke liy dard chhupate the ....
Mana, ishq me hadde nahi mappi jati magar ikkr toh maine
bhi kiya tha na,
Tum toh chal diye khair majbori meri rahi thi...
Samjhna chdh mann bhar gya kheh diye,
Itna hi pyr jataya tha shyd ki hum har gaye aur tum jeet
gaye...
Khehte hain sache pyar ki manzilen ni milti magar tum toh
afsaane de gaye !!

Sumedha walia

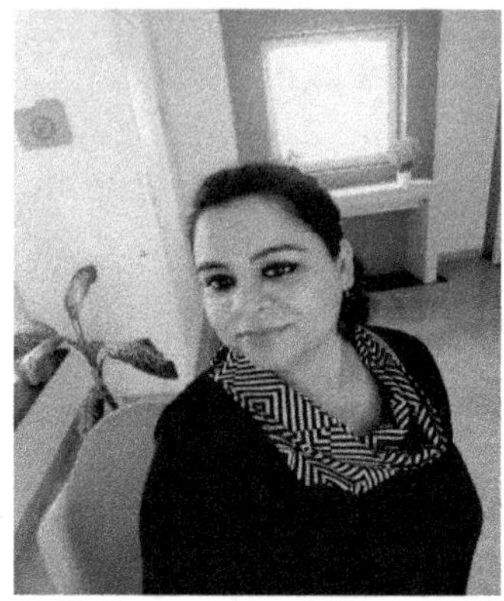

Sumedha describes herself as a girl who has lived quite a few chapters of her life. She is a voracious reader and lover of life .She now weaves her thoughts from those experiences. Bold & expressive with an endearing take on the shackles which encumber our society and stories which remained unfinished due to trepidation - nicely characterises her writings. Her quotes,poems are refreshingly upbeat and leave her readers with the question, what if. Uses her words to spread positivity and would exhort you to find the courage and maybe wings to fly. She lives each day to fullest and weaves her poems and stories with the moments she dreams or experiences.

\

That evening in the garden,

Where flowers were blooming in the spring.
That cool breeze flowing in full swing.
All you wanted was to see me smile.
You were teasing from a quite while.
At last I gave up tears and pretending
I cheered and smiled back withstanding
I couldn't thank enough to my stars.
Surely there were some faded scars.
But had you at disposal,
Everytime wanted to cry , laugh and to feel special.
You made me feel crazy and dizzness ,
With your anger and tenderness.
Thanks for being what your are.
Not mine, but still the knight in shining armour.
I don't know what is love.
But standing by you is quite enough.

Dim star

I was a dim star you made me bright
You are my Sun who is giving me light

Hold my hands let's walk in the starry night
Don't leave thread from ur hand as I am ur kite

I have some dreams, wanna see them with you
Most of the dreams are fulfilled as I found you

One of them is travelling together
Not only this world wanna cross with u heaven's ladder

We'll together walk miles
And be each other smiles

We will share abound so magnificent
Where materialistic things will not have any significance

Love is all that we share
Care and understanding are our treasure

When we have found each other
We will find the map which we want to travel

The only thing that's so perfect
Is how imperfectly we fit together.

Rashmika Aitha

Rashmika is a voracious consumer of the written word, who always has a book (or a Kindle, keeping with times) by her side that she devours. She is, a student aiming to reach the peak and have a glimpse once. Rashmika moonlights as a blogger where her nostalgic side seeps through her words. She is inclined towards micro tales and poems but secretly harbours a dream of writing a novel.

My Lifeline

I called out loud
From the mountain top
Hoping you won't go
You would turn around, stop.

And my shouts died
Into faint whispers
When you pretended
To turn deaf ears.

Ask the nights
How long I cried
And ask the sun
That couldn't give me life.
Ask my soul
How hard it tried
And to myself
How much I lied.
Is this the fate
Of every love story
Who think that
Everything is for eternity?
Or am I the one lost girl
Who never had it all?
Do I have an answer?
Or is it a question forever?

Kalamkaar

This is Kalamkaar. He is from Uttrakhand bought up in Meerut(Up). His hobbies are reading and writing. His interest is in writing. He love writing. He is part of 295 +Anthologies as Co-Author. He won 290 + Certificate in Writing, He Start writing 29 February 2020. He is part of 2 anthology as Co Author going for record and He is omg record holder as Co -Author of Book Called Laposia. He is part of 5 international Anthologies as Co - Author. He is simple and people observer. His insta handle is kalamkaar51 and email is kalamkaar51@gmail.com. He believes in Karma.

प्यार का तोहफा

जब कभी हम मिलते थे, बात खूब किया करते थे

हर जगह शहर मैं घुमते थे।

वक़्त हम बिताते थे

काम ऑफिस का रहता था उस एकदिन ही मुझे मिलने का मौका मिलता था।

मेहेंगा तोहफ़े की जरुरत नहीं थी हमें जो बिताते साथ हम वक़्त वही होता था हमारा प्यार का तोहफा।

बातभी इतवार के दिन हम खूब किया करते थे

उस छूटी के दिनको हम उनके साथ जिया करते थे

तू तड़ाक नहीं आप कहकर हम उनको सम्भोदित किया करते थे।

वो भी हमसे आप से ही सम्भोदित करती थी

हम उनको आप कहते वो हमको आप कहने से रोकती थी

हम उनसे कहते के अपने क्यों हमें आपको आप कहने से रोका।

क्योकि रिश्ते मे मेहेंगी चीज़े नहीं सम्मान देना होता हैं, अपने हमसफऱ को सबसे कीमती प्यार का तोहफा।

हम उनको खोने से नहीं डरते थे, जान अपनी छिड़कते थे

उनसे मिलने के लिए घड़ी की एक एकमिनट को गिनते थे

करले बात अगर किसी और मर्द से किसी जलसे मे मुस्कुराकर तो नहीं जलता था

भरोसा उसकी सच्चाई पार करता था, और किसी को बोलने का नहीं देता था मौका

भरोसा करना अपने हमसफर पर होता हैं, प्यार का सबसे हसीन तोहफा।

Laxmi Mondal

Laxmi Mondal is a 17 year old Science student . She loves loves writing poems and quotes , it's her passion .She has been a part of a anthology - "Isolating with our minds" .She is an aspiring writer . Till now she had been posting her writings on Instagram @visceral_soul_

DIL HI TOH HAI

Pyar toh har tarah ka hota hai
Koi jata ke karta hai , aur koi mann mein
Koi bata ke karta hai , aur koi durr se
Kisika pyaar unke karib hota hai , aur kisika bas unki yaadoin
mein
Woh pyaar jo yaadoin mein masboot rahe
Woh pyaar jiski khusboo durr se bhi mehekti hai
Uss pyaar ka bhi apna alag maza hai
Apna hi dard hai , aur apna gaana hai
Jo akele rehke bhi akele nhi rehne dete ...

COLOURS OF LOVE

Don't fall in love until it makes you rise
It should make you smile , even in your eyes
It should set you free , but still hold you close
It should give you wings ,not just a red rose
Love heals your scar , love hugs your pain
Love becomes your shed in the winter's rain
Love is about two souls ,
walking hand in hand
as calm as the water , seeping in through the sand .

A JOURNEY THROUGH LIFE

I was sitting by the lake waiting for him to arrive ,
thinking what could be the reasons for him to leave me .
Years passed by since we had last met .
But even now I think that we just met last night talking to
ourselves .

The golden sun was begin to set itself from
the infinite complexity of the galaxy
down to a simple night sky with
stars shimmering as the night dawns in .

I still wait for him in a hope that a day will come when
I will get an answer to my question .
But the day shall be far .
I think so as it is not a matter of time but a journey through
life midway .

Srijani Das

Srijani is currently studying in class 11, lives in West Bengal,
Favourite hobbies include reading and writing
Instagram - @shit_i_am_unknown_

Love or should I say foolish hope

"Sanyukta", A black haired girl with red spectacles on her brown coloured eyes turned around at the sound of her name being called. Swati, her one and only Friend waved at her as she stood near the door of their examination hall. Sanyukta turning her eyes towards her book approached her friend with small steps. Swati, turning impatient shoved her inside the examination room. 'BANG!', Sanyukta laid flat on the floor with someone under her. She quickly got up and sat on her assigned sit without looking elsewhere. After the exam Swati and the other girls got busy teasing her with her romantic accident before exam. One whispered excitedly, " 'Sanyu' did you managed to write all the answers correctly or were you too excited to recall anything..." "Well I heard Souryadeep is still single, you can have your try". Sanyukta would have ignored them but unfortunately Souryadeep was her childhood crush whom she has already decided was her Prince charming unknown to the others. Sanyukta, who's face was red from embarrassment turned her head towards Swati in hope for some help. Swati was busy eyeing someone among the group of boys on the other side of the class. Sanyukta followed Swati's line of vision and spotted Souryadeep. The embarrassing smile vanished from her face and she was back to her aloof self and ignored the other girls until they got tired of teasing her and left. It was not long before Swati excitedly announced that she and Souryadeep started dating. Swati's words were, "Although he is not my type and I don't like him that much, he is better than the other idiots I dated before, so why don't I give it a try."
This is what happened 6 years ago. Now Sanyukta is a practising doctor at a renowned hospital and have lost connections with Swati since they enrolled in different University. Swati and Souryadeep broke up during high

school. Sanyukta who finally got rid of her introvert self is now a successful person with a cheerful, carefree, kind and adventurous personality. Everyone around her seems to fall in love with her.

Well it is sometimes true when you say that the world is a small place. Sanyukta was not ready to find Souryadeep looking up at her from where he lead on the floor of the hospital as she looked down at him from her position above him. Warm hopes of forgotten feelings was felt by Sanyukta as the sound of her frantic heartbeat filled her ears.

Yatri patel

She is a yatri she is a science student she live in gujrat she interested in writing she love to write poem

तुझ से इश्क करना चाहती हूं

हा में इश्क करना चाहती हूं
तेरे साथ कुछ पल बिताना चाहती हूं
इश्क में लगे ज़ख्म तुम्हे दिखाना चाहती हूं
हा में तुझ से इश्क करना चाहती हूं
तेरे आंखो के आंसु अपनी आंखो से गिराना चाहती हूं
तुझे लगे हर घाव का मरहम बनना चाहती हूं
हा तुझ से इश्क करना चाहती हूं
तेरी हर मुस्कान कि वजह बनना चाहती हूं
तेरी खामोशी को पढ़ना चाहती हूं
हा तुझ से इश्क करना चाहती हूं
तेरे इश्क में पागल बन कर घूमना चाहती हूं
हीर रांझा राधाकृष्ण के जैसे अपनी कहानी बनाना चाहती हूं
हा तुझ से इश्क करना चाहती हूं
देर रात जग कर तुझ से बाते करना चाहती हूं
प्यार मोहब्बत की उन कसमो को खाना चाहती हूं
हा तुझ से में इश्क करना चाहती हूं
जुदाई का प्यारा सा दर्द सेहना चाहती हूं
तेरी यादों में पूरी रात रोना चाहती हूं
हा तुझ से इश्क करना चाहती हूं
प्यार कि राहों में तेरे साथ चलना चाहती हूं
तुझ से कदम से कदम मिला ना चाहती हूं
हा तुझ से इश्क करना चाहती हूं
सबके सामने तेरे साथ सात फेरे लेना चाहती हूं
उन सात कसमो को जीना चाहती हूं
हा तुझ से इश्क करना चाहती हूं

Niva Patra

Niva Patra is from Bhopal, (M.P). She is a graphics designer and animation illustrator also a practising CA, formerly worked as a project manager in advertising platforms. she is a writer by day and a reader by night, also Co-author of many anthologies. She is a district level debator and won many achievements for her poems and stories. Motivation is the key, the society, things happening around her, especially her imagination power motivates her to write more and more. It's almost as good as a conversation. Follow her on Instagram @artistic_pen_stories and @niva_patra .

COMPLICATED CONFUSED LOVE

Love like you comes only in movies,
Our lips pressed together,
The art of making love,
Ur hands on my back,
All these makes me feel…uh are only mine,
Although I know…it's not true!!!
We can't be together always,
Coz' neither you love me,
Nor your society would accept.
Still I want you babe!!!
Your touch makes me feel so divine!!!
Now I seems to be an end…
Happy marriage love!!!!

काश यह बस मे मेरे होता

हम-तुम से हमसफर बन जाते,
तुमसे बात करने का बहाना मिल जाता,
मिलते तुम, तो किस्मत को खजाना मिल जाता,
काश यह बस मे मेरे होता।।

कौन कहता हैं...
कौन कहता हैं... सिर्फ़ इज़्हार ही प्यार होता हैं,
कभी सच्ची मोहब्बत मे इंतज़ार करा हैं,
यह भी मोहब्बत की तालीम हैं,
जनाब, कल्पना मे रहना भी आशिक़ की जिन्दगी का हिस्सा हैं।।

Ms. Ishrat Jahan Noor mohammed khan

Ms Ishrat jahan khan is a passionate Teacher and a Writer she loves reading and writing. Loving and caring is her hobby. And keep learning and accept the positive suggestion is her quality.

She belongs to North India and stays at Ulhasnagar (Maharashtra).

Loves humanity always instagram - @ishrat7755

Pyar ka ehsaas

Pyar ka ehsaas hota
Jindagi ka abhaas hota
Dard bahot hote hai
Par pyar par viswas hote hai

Koi kitna bhi pyar kare
Koi kitna bhi inkaar kare
Pyar ka rista ajeeb hota hai
Dur wahi hota hai jo kareeb hota hai

Humdard ban jaate hai kuch pal may
Bedard ban jaate kuch pal may
Aasan nahi hota ye pyar
Ismay bhi hote hai takraar....

It's Complicated

Love is difficult
It is very cult
We need compassion
And they want passion

Love is a care
Where we always dare
But it's without fear
As you are dear

It's very hurting
When your partner is flirting
You were behind true love
They felt its a namesake love

Love is very delicated
Yes friends it's complicated....

Sanjay Naik

Sanjay Naik is from Kharagpur State of West Bengal. He is an Economics graduate (Hons), a writer from the heart and passionate about singing.
Through the platform of anthology, he wants to spread love & positivity among his readers and wants to heal his readers' hearts with his magical words.

Sanjay is at utmost peace when he pens his emotions. He believes that the power of his words, will heal the wounds of many readers.

ONE SIDED LOVE !!

I do not know how to live without you
I am trying to be worthy of you
Only your name is written in my soul ,
in my life
Your presence makes me relaxed
Can't show you my pain
Your lack keeps torturing me every day .

This love of mine is one sided
In which my devotion have no boundaries
You are oblivious to my pain and love
I want to express my feelings
But your refusal can shock the heart .

I secretly watch you
If you see, I steal my eyes from you
My life seems to be a love affair
I have started knitting you
unnecessarily in my dreams
I started listening a lot without you saying
Now how can I tell the secret of my heart ??

हमसफ़र !!

इसे विधि का विधान समझूं
या कुदरत का इशारा समझूं
प्यार को सिर आंखों पर रखी तूने मेरी
मर्यादा से सुसज्जित ऐसी वो दीवार समझूं।

इसे अपने मन में अंकित कोई वहम समझूं
या छुपा हुआ मेरा उज्ज्वल भविष्य समझूं
एक आधार रखी है आश्रय को तूने मेरी
अभिलाषाओं की ऐसी वो द्वार समझूं।

इसे तेरा बड़प्पन समझूं या
जल अर्पित करने वाली पवित्र
कोई कलश समझूं
मायने मिल गए हैं मन्नतों को मेरे
मेरे हसरतों की तुझे वो सारी
जागीर समझूं।

Sanoj kumar

He is an engineer, started writing two years back never imagined that people would like it, and feel his emotions as theirs. He also likes to express other's feelings and always try to change other's mindsets in a better way through his writings. Nowadays he is a member of many writing communities and earned lots of certificates through his writings. His first book as an author named in hindi "Safar-Zindagi Ka "and he also works on many anthologies as compiler and editor. Currently, he is a co-author approx 50 anthologies. If you want to know more then simply type safarzindagikask in Google.

तन्हा हूं

तन्हा हूं मैं, तेरे बिना,
भीड़ में भी ढूंढ़ू, तू है कहां।
जिन्दगी के इस दौर में,
मैं यहां और तू है वहां।

तेरे गलियों में मारा फिरता हूं,
तेरी ही खुशबू में खोया रहता हूं।
जहां कभी हमने प्यार के पल बिताए थे,
वहां आज में आशुं बहाया करता हूं।

अकेला हूं, फिर भी तेरा ही सहारा है,
तेरे सिवा और कोई ना मुझे गवारा है।
कठिन से कठिन परिस्थितियों में भी
हर वक़्त तूने ही तो मुझे सँवरना है।

तेरी गजरे की महक की कमी खलती है,
अब कैंटीन के पीछे कहां तुम मिलती है।
मां बहन ने मेरे लिए लड़की भी ढूंढ ली,
पर तेरे सामने किसी ओर कि कहां चलती है।

Jaya Bhardwaj

जया भारद्वाज पेशेवर रूप से एक सॉफ्टवेयर इंजीनियर हैं। वो बताती हैं कि उन्हें लिखना बहुत पसंद है। उन्होंने वर्ष 2013 में लेखन कार्य शुरू किया, जब उन्होंने अपने कौशल को पहचाना था। वे बताती हैं, कि आनुवंशिक रूप से उन्होंने इस आदत को प्राप्त किया है। उनके पिता "श्री श्याम शर्मा" को मुशायरा सुनना और विभिन्न कवियों की कवितायें पढ़ना बहुत अच्छा लगता था और वे हिंदी साहित्य में भी खास रूचि रखते थे। आपकी प्रतिभाशाली लेखनी ने आज हमें आपसे जुड़ने का मौका दिया। आप अपने प्रयासों में सफल हो हम ऐसी कामना करते हैं।

<u>क्या आज भी जिंदा हो तुम।</u>

क्या कहीं आज भी जिंदा हो तुम मेरे बग़ैर,
मुझसे कोसों दूर ।
तो क्या कहीं आज भी जिंदा हो तुम ।
तो शायद, तुम्हारे वो वादे भी सब ख्याली थे।
इसलिए शायद, मेरे जज़्बात भी उस वक्त सवाली थे ।
एक वक्त था जब कुछ तो था, दरमियान अपने ।
क्योंकि तुम्हीं मेरी होली थे, तुम्हीं दिवाली थे ।
तो क्या कहीं आज भी जिंदा हो तुम।
पर अब न है तुझसे दूर जाने का ग़म।
क्योंकि हो गया है मुझे एहसास अब।
कि एक उम्र का तकाजा़ था, और हम-तुम भी मवाली थे ।
तो क्या कहीं आज भी जिंदा हो तुम।
उन जिंदा दफ़न ख्यालों के साथ,
जो करते थे इक वक्त पर इस रिश्ते की रखवाली थे ।
क्योंकि हम-तुम भी,
एक वक्त पर आशिक और मवाली थे।
तो क्या कहीं आज भी जिंदा हो तुम।

मैंने तुझको चुना होगा जब

मैंने तुझको चुना होगा जब,
बस तुम मुझसे क्यों ना पूछना।
नहीं बता पाऊंगी मैं, क्या ख्याल उस वक्त मेरे ज़हन में आया होगा।
शायद तेरा अंदाज़, तेरे अल्फ़ाज़, तेरा मिज़ाज मुझे भाया होगा।
बक्शीश ए ख़ुदा समझकर ही शायद मैंने तुझे अपनाया होगा।
बस तुम मुझसे क्यों ना पूछना,
क्या ख्याल उस वक्त मेरे ज़हन में आया होगा।
मान लिया था तुम्हें हमदर्द, हमराही, हमनवां।
क्या पता था कुछ वक्त के लिए ही तेरा साया होगा।
क्योंकि अब जो तुम मेरे साथ नहीं,
तो शायद उस ख़ुदा ने भी अपनी अधूरी लिखी कहानी में पूर्ण विराम लगाया होगा।
और उसका भी दिल भर आया होगा ।
बस तुम मुझसे क्यों ना पूछना, जब मैंने तुम्हें चुना था।
क्या ख्याल उस वक्त मेरे ज़हन में आया होगा ।

Roohi Prasad

She is Roohi, a student
Writing is her passion and
her love is her strength

ये मोहब्बत

नशा है या है जुनून ये मोहब्बत
शौक है या है चाहत ये मोहब्बत...
हकीकत भी हकीकत न लगे
जाने कैसी बला है ये मोहब्बत...
वहम इसके होने का ही सही
वहम में भी हसीन है ये मोहब्बत...
सोचा था भेजी दुआ है खुदा की
अब जाना है कि खुदा है मोहब्बत...

नशा

नशा शराब का करो या नशा मोहब्बत का करो
फर्क सिर्फ इतना ही है की
शराब का नशा मोहब्बत लगते ही उतर जाता है
और मोहब्बत का नशा उतारे नहीं उतरता

Neha Raghav

DR.Neha Raghav from ghaziabad,uttarpradesh.She is a sports physiotherapist.her hobbies is writing and observing peoples.

हक

तूने मेरी हर बात पर हक जताया था,
क्या सही है क्या गलत है मुझे सब बताया था,
बहुत गलतियां करती हो तुम यह बार-बार कह के,
तूने मुझे तुझ पर विश्वास करना सिखाया था,
तूने मेरी हर बात पर हक जताया था,

हा, तूने मेरे हर वक्त मेरा साथ दिया,
मेरी लिखने की आदत को नया आकार दिया,
मेरी जिंदगी पर सारे के सारे हक तेरे हो गए थे,
मगर अपनी बड़ी तो छोड़ तूने कोई छोटी बात कभी पता ना लगने दिया,
वह पल बहुत खूब था जब मैंने तुझसे धक्का खाया था,
तूने मेरी हर बात पर हक जताया,

किसी ने कहा कि तूने इतने भी हक नहीं दिए थे मुझे कि मैं तेरी जिंदगी में दखल दे जा ऊ,
तेरे हर फैसले में खुद से बोल जाऊ
पर अब क्या बताऊं उसे की मेरा दर्जा कहा था,
बोल जायेंगे सच क्युकी
क्युकी मुझे सच पर यकीन करना भी तूने सिखाया था,
तूने मेरी हर बात पर हक जताया था।

Ipsita Panigrahi

A carefree, joyful, realistic in practical life but she enjoys to live in an imaginative and fictional world. This is Ipsita Panigrahi, a budding writer, who loves to express her feelings and emotions through writings. She hails from Bhubaneswar -the city of temples, Odisha. She has a passion for literature, as she loves to do all those stuff which makes her happy and literature is one among them. She is likely to be called as a scribbler. She finds peace in gardening and reading books and an artist is also hidden in her.

Love is Love...!!!

Love is not just a word of emotions.
It's full of dedication and appreciation.

The person whom you love ,is the person whom we adore the most.
And you promise yourself
And to your bond that you are not going to give up ,
No matter how much the situation becomes worse.

No matter how many scars and flaws you have.
Your love will make his own ave.
Just be the way ,the way you are .
One day for sure your love will make you his life's gleaming star.

Love is eternal .
It tastes like the coconut sweet kernel.
Love's dictionary has no what called depart .
It never allows you to become a part of the rife,
And ceases all the strife between the mind and heart.

The more you dive into .
The more you will be explored to.
The more you are poured with love .
The less you are implored like the dove.

Over the dreams and creams.
Whether you smile or scream.
It will truly abide .
And make your miseries short and happiness wide.

It will never dare to leave you alone .
It will behave as if it's your clone.

No matter in cheers or tears.
It will stay for years and years.

Through the ups and downs ,
Through the ridges furrows.
He will never dim your grace even through the sorrows.

It will always remain side by side .
Even after your death your soul will unite.

Pankaj Sharma

Panka Sharma is student now
He is preparing for gorvment job Special for army Likhna suru kiya jab main 10 class me tha jab meri pahli baar breakup huyi thi ek ladki ke saath jise main bahut pyaar karta tha

Kya wo pyaar tha

Jab collage ke din maine pahli baar tumhe dekha .to aisa lga meri puri zindagi ek si ho gayi hai .main aur mere do dost thik tumhaare saamne secound brench pr baithe the .kha se main tumhe dekh saku.sir jor jor se kuch padhane ki kosis kar rahe the .lekin tumhaari dhadkno ki awaaj se unki awaaj kahi gum si ho jaati thi .kya wo pyaar tha .mujhe nahi aata pyaar ka ijhaar karna .kaash tum aankho ki bhasa samajh leti .main kuch kahna chah rha tha .par kuch kah nahi paaya .dil me kuch baat thi jo juba par aati thi .par lafjo par aate aate kahi kho si jaati thi .kya wo pyaar tha .aankho se aankhe mil gayi baato se baatein mil gayi .aur wo mulaaqate dheere2 pyaar me badal gayi.tab tumne ek baat kahi thi .pankaj ladki ka haath kabhi bhihaatho me haath pakad kar rakhte hai .main man hi man muskura kr yah kah gya ki main tumhaara haath zindagi bhar pakad kr rakhna chahta hu .kya wo pyaar tha .us din se padhayi ke liye collage jaana .bekaar sa lagta tha .aur jis din tum nahi aati us din pura collage bekaar sa lagta tha .tab se tum meri zindagi ka hissa ban gayi .in aankho ko teri aadat si ho gayi thi .in otho ko teri ibaadat si ho gayi thi .suno n babu kya wo pyaar tha .

Suno n babu kya wo pyaar tha .pyar tha ya kuch aur tha lekin babu jo bhi tha wo tumse hi tha ....my love raadhika special for u

Divyanshi Goel

Divyanshi Goel is a first year student of Bansthali Vidhyapeeth and currently taking up a bachelor's degree in Psychology. She completed her school life in Ryan International School. Divyanshi, a potent poet and mother of tolerating other people, sits in her dreamy state and observe the world so closely that they somehow end up on pages of her diary. She always walking into new worlds through her favourite songs while being inspired by them and inspiring others. The compatible best friend for everyone and a dreamer of poetries. Her insta poetries account is @apeiron_fiction.

"YOU

I fell for you;
I had no clue..!!
That someday you will be my rue,
And my heart was going to be screwed..!!

Feelings were true,
Yet they were off no use..!!
Cause it was like huge blew,
Where sound of boom is mute..!!

The million chats were vanished,
In the unknown pin drop silence..!!
I felt isolated,
Feeling inside I was struggling with violence..!!

There was no bickering,
Just me, he and crying.
Where both souls were dying;
And pretending to be just fine..!!

That was our love,
Undefined toxic and rough..!!
It wasn't good , it wasn't bad enough;
Just our stories which was really tough..!!!

Diksha Motwani

Diksha is a passionate girl from Mumbai, Maharashtra. She loves to pen her feelings. She is introvert but her pen makes her extrovert. She is a writer, singer, artist and a poet!

Still am waiting!_

You promised that you will be back very soon,
But you didnt,
I attempted to forget you as you were may be a boon,
But I didnt!

Yes, you are still my morning's first thought,
Yes, I still adore you,
Yes, I still love you.
But may be now, I will not have you.

You were my blooming moon,
You were my shine of darkest days,
unfortunately, you are not mine now,
Yet I still wait for you every single day!

Kiruthika C

She is C.kiruthika aged 23. She have completed M.A., English literature in Nandha Arts and science college, Affiliated under Bharathiar University Coimbatore,Tamilnadu. She had translated short stories. She wrote more than 30 stories. Her aim is to be a writer and lecturer.

FEAR OF LOVE

Daily I used to see more people. I had crossed many persons in my life. Many persons are loving truly and some persons are loving for enjoyment. This made me very irritating towards love. I heard a bitter experience from my friend side. So that I was in very afraid of love.

Mehta and Haswanth are lovers. They are loving more than eight years. Between them, there was no quarreling and separation. This made everyone of their friends said they were a ever loving couples. This made Mehta and Haswanth to be too happy.

They completed their college and they got a degree. After that they went to job. This promotes them to fell inferiority complex between them. They argue more at sometimes for something. This made them separation. Mehta felt too agony. She doesn't bare Haswanth's reaction.

According to him he wish to leave her. Do he uttered bad words with lot of scolding. This made Mehta to became anger towards Haswanth. He suspected her behavior too. These things made irritated and Mehta felt to leave him as his wish.

Likewise she done. She didn't speak to Haswanth for three months. Haswanth forgotten her and he loves another girl named Ashika. Whole hearing thus Mehta felt very same and she feel bad for loving such kind of person.

Luckily she escaped from him. After that she hate marriage and she didn't accept marriage life. She lost her hope. She runs the charitable trust for orphanage. And she adopted two children and lead a happy life. Whereas Haswanth became mad because the girl whom he loved left him after getting all his wealth.

Mehta took care him too in the orphanage. She cared him like other children. On seeing such activities I had a fear in

love and marriage. This type of incident made me to fear."LOVE IS FAITH WE SHOULDN'T DROP OUR HEARTS IF WE DROP WE MAY FACE CERTAIN PROBLEMS ".

Priyanka Sharma

She is a student Of B.A..
She struggling Writing and Acting..
She loves to do Audio Poetries and Video Editing..
She want to fulfill her dreams. She wants to be a successful girl in our life..

अनकही यादों के अल्फ़ाज़

1. हर पल मैं तुझे याद करा करती हूँ,
ना जाने तु कहाँ खो गया,
अक्सर मैं तेरा इंतजार करा करती हूँ,
थोड़ा वक्त हमारे साथ भी निभा लिया करो,
दो पल की जिंदगी कभी भी अपना मोड़ बदल सकती है,
इसलिए हमेशा तेरी तस्वीर को देख कर तुझे याद करा करती हूँ।।।

2. इन टिमटिमाती रातों में तुम्हारी यादे तड़पाती है,
तुम कहाँ खो गए इस भीड़ में,
हमें तो आज भी तुम्हारी पुरानी बातें सताती है।।।

3. वो कहता है मुझसे मोहब्बत नहीं है मुझे तुमसे,
पर उसकी ये बात मेरे समझ नहीं आती हैं,
मेरे हर दर्द पर वो क्यों रोता है यही बात मुझे हमेशा सताती है।।।

4. नहीं समझ पाता कोई मुझे आजकल,
क्यों कि सब सुनते मेरे अल्फ़ाज़ हैं,
अल्फ़ाज़ों में बहुत दर्द हैं मेरे,
मगर हर शब्द के पीछे एक गहरा राज़ हैं।।।
5. तु किधर चला जाता है,
तेरा जाना मुझे बहुत सताता है,
तु मुझे इतना तड़पाता है,
फिर भी ये दिल तुझ ही को चाहता है।।।

6. कुछ नहीं बस महफ़िलों में बैठे थे हम,
उस रोनक के बीच हमने भी थोड़ा मुस्कुरा दिया,
कुछ बातें वो अपने दिल पर ले गए फिर उन्होंने हमें अपने दिल से निकाल दिया,

इन महफिलों की बातों की उलझनों में हमने उन्हें इस कदर खो दिया।।।

7. क्या लिखूँ मैं तेरे लिए तु तो खुद मेरी एक शायरी है, तेरी यादों में मैं इस कदर गुम हो गई हूँ,
के लिखे हुए अल्फाजों को भी मैं भूल गई हूँ।।।

Chandni Kesharwani

An entrepreneur by profession Chandni Kesharwani holds Masters of Child Psychology.She feels privileged to live in different cities around the world and that gave her opportunity to make friends from all walks of life and different nationalities.She want to establish as a motivational poet and writer.Presently she is very active on social media platforms and her motivational quotes on life have been liked by many people.She has written Two Anthology before.She presently lives in Gurgaon, Haryana.

Instagram - hindi_sahityakar

E mail : chandni.kesharwani1981@gmail.com

।।दिलों की आहट।।

चलो आज फिर से दिलों की,
आहट सुन आए हम।
चंचल किरणों की थोड़ी,
शरारत सुन आए हम।
चलो भीनी- भीनी रातों में,
फूलों की गुनगुनाहट सुन आए हम ।
चलो आज फिर से,
दिलों की आहट सुन आए हम ।
मस्तानी रातों में ,
चांद तारों की बारात सजा लाए हम।
सूने से आंगन में,
प्यार का दीप जला आए हम ।
जुगनू की रोशनी में,
चलो सेज सजा आए हम।
चलो आज फिर से,
दिलों की आहट सुन आए हम।
अपने प्यार का,
इक नया गीत गुनगुना आए हम ।
प्रेमियों के मन में,
इक नई उम्मीद जगा आए हम।
खिलते फूलों की,
थोड़ी खुशबू चुरा लाएं हम ।
चलो आज फिर से,
दिलों की आहट सुन आए हम।

Gautam Saini

Gautam saini is from Karnal, Haryana.
He currently opt medicine as academics and running instagram page @the_writerdesk. He is a Gold medalist in Science Olympiad and 2nd Runner up in KOCA(World's Biggest Youth fest). He loves to do writing, acting, vlogging, teaching, singing. He writes because he felt that it is the bestway to explore ourself and it makes him remind of halcyon days.

दामन से कफ़न तक का सफर

कुछ सवाल जेहन में तंग बहुत करते है,
लोगों को लगता है हम जिया करते है, पर उन्हें कौन बताए
हम वो आशिक़ है जो कब्र मै भी रोज़ मरा करते है।
अब भरी महफ़िल में अपनी मौत का इंतजाम ख़ुद ही किया करता
हूं,
एक दो जाम को छोड़, पूरी बोतल खाली किया करता हूं।
कैसी कश्मकश है ये उनसे बिना मिले भी, बात उन्ही की कर रहा
हूं,
हालत परिंदे जैसी होगी है पिंजरे से निकल तो गया, पर फिर भी मर
रहा हूं।
तुम्हारा शहर अभी भी मुझे अपना माना करता है,
शायद वो ही जो हमारी दूरियों को सही मापा करता है।
अपने दिल के टुकड़ों को समेटता हूं तो हर बार तुम ही मिल जाती
हो,
सुना है मेरे दिए हुए तोफो को तुम बाज़ार में बेच आती हो।
महसूस जो किया था मैने वो गैरो का इतर था क्या,
कल जिससे मिली थी वो हमसे भी अच्छा मित्र था क्या।
मेरे प्यार के दामन को तुम कफ़न बना कर जा रही हो,
बड़ी खुश लग रही हो लगता है किसी नए आशिक़ से मिल कर आ
रही हो।

Nagma Tarannum

Her name is Nagma Tarannum.
She is a science student.
She is a writer who writes her heart out and describe her self.
She wants to make her parents proud by her work.
She likes to do designing clothes and also she sing well.
Bold personality with soft-hearted nature.

एक इल्तेजा

बहुत कुछ है तुमसे कहना
तुम वक्त निकाल कर कभी तो सुनना
हो अगर खफा तो बयां करना
मेरा इतना सा हक तो अदा करना
अपनी दिवानगी की दलील न दे सकूंगी
मेरे अल्फाजों पर ही तुम यकीं करना
मेरे इज्तिराब की कोई तो तहलील अता करना
मेरी बेबसी का कुछ तो ख्याल करना
ख्वाबिदा है जहान मेरा
मेरे ख्वाबों का कुछ तो लिहाज करना
मयस्सर अगर हो वक्त तुम्हारा
मुकम्मल मेरी बस ये इल्तेजा करना

कुर्बत

तेरी कुर्बत में मेरा खुद को खो देना
तेरे बिना मेरा हर लम्हा रो देना
मेरी हर खुशी में तेरा हिस्सा होना
तेरे बिना मेरी जिंदगी बस एक किस्सा होना
मेरी हर ख्वाहिश में तेरा जिक्र रहना
हर वक़्त मेरे लबों पर बस तेरी फिक्र रहना
तेरी खुशबु से मेरा महक उठना
तेरी आवाज से मेरा चहक उठना
मेरी हर दुआ में तेरा नाम होना
तेरे ख्यालों में खोना बस एक यही मेरा काम होना
तेरी बातो का बस एतबार करना
तुझे खोने से मेरा हर बार डरना
तेरी एक झलक को मेरा बेकरार रहना
तुझे देख ही मेरा सुकून से सांस लेना
अगर होती भी है तो हो जाये फनाह दुनिया सारी
ख्वाहिश है तो बस तू मेरा रहे और मेरी जिंदगी तेरे नाम होना

Adarsh Singh

आदर्श सिंह एक नई पीढ़ी के रचनाकार है। इनका जन्म कानपुर में हुआ है। वर्तमान में यह दिल्ली से 'बैचलर ऑफ जर्नलिज्म एंड मास कम्युनिकेशन' की पढ़ाई कर रहे है। इनकी कविताएं समसमायिक घटनाओं से लेकर भावनात्मकता से प्रेरित होती है। एक कविता से यह यात्रा प्रारंभ हुई और अभी गतिमान है।

प्रस्तुत कविता लड़का, लड़की और उनके संदर्भों को बयान करती एक प्रेम यात्रा है।

मैं, कक्षा और तुम

हरी कुर्ती काली सलवार पहन वो नंगे पैर मेरी कक्षा में चली आयी थी,

ज़िन्दगी में पहली बार उसने ही तो मेरी नजर किसी पर रुकवाई थी,

मुझे देख मन ही मन तो वो भी मुस्कराई थी,

मेरे पूछने पर उसने खुद को मुझसे एक कक्षा बड़ी बतलाई थी,

मेरी कक्षा में तो बस वो मास्टर जी से हाजरी लगवाने आयी थी,

बात जब इश्क की आयी थी,

तब दोनों की कक्षा बीच में आयी थी,

बहाने से वो मुझसे मिलने आया करती थी,

वो मुलाकाते कब दोस्ती में बदल गई ये सोच किसने लगाई थी,

जब ओढ़ने वाले थे हम इश्क की वो रजाई थी,

तब उसकी पढ़ाई पूरी हो चली आयी थी,

अब वो कॉलेज से चली गई थी,

हमारी प्रेम कहानी जिस कक्षा से शुरू हुई थी,

अब उसी कक्षा में गुमनाम हो चुकी थी।

Jaya Chandana Medidhi

Jaya Chandana Medidhi, is a postgraduate from Andhra university. She is a nature and animal lover. She's an introvert to express her feelings, which made her way to pen down to express her feelings. Her writings include family emotions, destiny, happiness.

LOVE OF ATHEESHAN

ATHEESHAN – THE MIGHTY TREE
Many years ago, there was a jungle full of giant trees and the head is ATHEESHAN, the mightiest of all, and king of trees. It was a sacred and medicinal one too. Soon, the essence of Atheeshan went out of the forest to tribes later to nearby villages. People began to come to Atheeshan and see him, to pluck the tastiest fruits of that tree.

Later it grew to branches export due to its medicinal value, gradually a way was made from Atheeshan to worldwide in exports of its fruits, branches, wood, etc. People used to come for picnic, children use to play around him. There used to be fun around Atheeshan always. It provides shelter in sunny and even rainy days. It's the home for many birds, animals, small creatures. It's like the host of forest. Gradually it became a famous place in and around the forest.

Sooner, its branches are cutdown for benefits, and the day came that Atheeshan could not produce. Even though that mighty tree stood up for people in and around and still used to grew for others need and greed. It didn't stop giving out its freshness, its fruit to people who ask . Slowly, Atheeshan became old and started to wither, however gave his medicinal effects and sacredness to his children, those trees which grew beside him.

Atheeshan represents father in our lives. He is that one who grew older and older giving all this stuff to his children. Even though he is in such a painful situation, he just gives off his goodness and honour to his family. A father always thinks of his family and people who relies on him. Likewise, or Atheeshan too gave his good fruit to the one who relies on him for wood, fruits and benefits.

This Atheeshan mighty tree stood on behalf of the head of the family, FATHER.

Pooja Desai

Pooja Desai , Who born in State Karnataka , Gulbarga city is graduated. She believes that writing is the best way of expressing feeling. The feelings which cannot be shared , can be expressed through writing . Through her writing she wants to make an impact on readers and to be a ray of hope for the hopeless.

प्यार

मन किया प्यार दिया बिन कहे चल दिया
हमसे ना होगा ये सेहना ।
बोहोत रोलिया प्यार के भिक मांगकर ,
तुमसे अब कुछ न है केहना ।
राह तेरी देखती रही कि कब तुम मुजे अपनाओगे
पर रेह गया वो अधूरा सपना ।
दिन बीत गए तुम न आए ,
आदत बन गया तेरे यादों में जीना ।
अभी दोस्ती तुम्हे निभानी है प्यार को भूल जाना है ,
 इससे अच्छा तुम दुर ही रेहना ।
अब सारी शिकायतों का उत्तर मेरी खामोशी देगी सुन लेना ।

राह

कोई उसको बताए
कि मेरी राह पे चले आए
इंतजार का पल बीत गए
तरस रही है आंखे देखने केलिए
उसको कोई खबर दे आए

रिश्ते

रिश्ते भी अजीब होते है
कभी बातों बातों में
मिल जाते है तो,
कभी बिन बात किए
 टूट जाते है ।

SOUNDARYA MOHAN

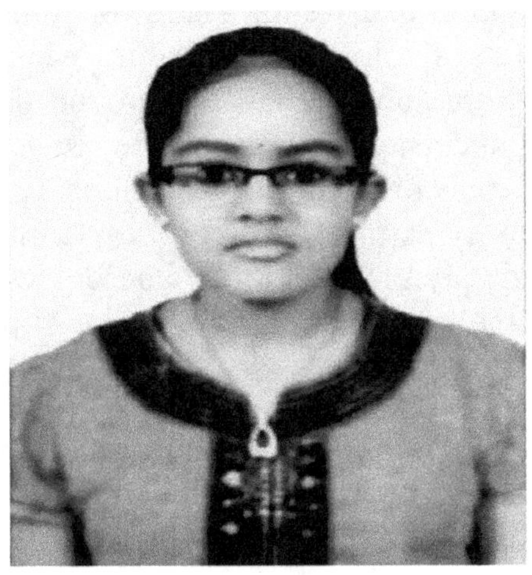

Soundarya Mohan is a College Student. She is a Third Year Undergraduate Student of Bachelor of Arts in Guru Nanak Khalsa College Matunga Mumbai. She lives in Sion Mumbai. She likes to Write and express out feelings. She is a Writer by passion, She Believes that Everyone must have a dream to achieve something in life. She is pursuing literature. She likes to Read and Write books, stories, novels, articles, poems etc. She is also a nature lover. She has won First prize in Intercollegiate Article Writing Competition. She likes to Read books a lot.

MOTHER'S LOVE.

Love is an Emotion that we all Yearn for right from the day we are born we crave love. Little babies who just enter this world are unaware about what goes around here. If there is one thing they understand it is love. They understand nothing else but love and crave for it. They long to be with their parents and family as they can feel the warmth and love by their touch and care. They hesitate and cry when a stranger picks them as the love quotient is lower or at times not there at all.

The Mother- Child Relationship is said to be the Strongest. The sole reason for it is love. There is immense love involved.

The Mother loves the child selflessly and the later reciprocates this love. A person with a kind and loving nature is loved by all. For instance, a teacher who is loving and supporting is loved by the students while one who is harsh is not liked by anyone. Similarly, we love those people who love us and treat us nicely. We look forward to meet them and feel happy in their company.

Thus, Love is the basis of every relationship. A Place Where People live with each other is Peaceful and Beautiful as True Soul Mates Made for Each other.

LOVE ISN'T ALWAYS PERFECT

True love is something so elusive that many refuse to accept that it exists. Their incredulity is understandable considering what a me-first world we live in. When people seek only to please themselves, they will never be capable of finding true love. True love is self sacrificing. True love is not blind to faults, but it is willing to look for the best in others, focus on their good qualities. True love is not principally about recieving, but rather true love looks for opportunities to give. True love between two people is the most precious of gifts. It is one of the few things left in this world that can endure an entire lifetime, for true love is stronger even than death.

It isn't a fairytale or a storybook. If doesn't always comes easy. Love is overcoming obstacles, facing challenges, fighting to be together, holding on and never letting go. It is a short word, easy to spell, difficult to define, and impossible to live without love. Love is Work, but Most of all, Love is realizing that you cannot stay without each other even for a while and knowing that every hour, every minute, and every second was worth it and Precious Because you did it Together.

Manas Pradhan

Manas Pradhan is from Diamond City of The India - Surat. He is studying in Class 11 at Gajera Vidyabhavan. He believes that being a Science student you can understand the world more so why just dig our eyes on books and projects, let's explore the wide..!! He have many hobbies like public speaking, writing, cooking, reading spiritual books, social and educational volunteering and many things, he want to do everything a student can do of other Streams also as he doesn't want to be limited but to experience the unlimited. But what motivated him to start writing?? Yes, everything starts with some uncertain works, as one fine day he was reading some shayaris, then something hit his mind and he penned down and got appreciation, and from then to now he is penning down his ink of thoughts.!!

तुमसे इश्क़

मेरी रूह ने उससे कहा,

"दूर रहकर भी लगता है
नजदीकियां बढ़ रही है!!

नफ़रत करके भी लगता है
लगाव बढ़ रहा है !!

क्या लग रहा है मुझे सिर्फ ऐसा
या कर रहे हों तुम भी एहसास..??

पता नहीं क्या खेल
खेल रहा है मेरा ये दिल!!

क्या हो रहा है
मुझे तुमसे इश्क़..??"

उसके दिल ने जवाब दिया,

"दूर मैं हूं
नज़दीक तुम रखलो!!

नफ़रत मैं करती हूं
लगाव तुम बढ़ालो!!

नहीं लग रहा तुम्हें सिर्फ ऐसा
हाँ कर रही हूं मैं भी एहसास!!

ये खेल तुम्हारें दिल का नहीं
मेरी रूह का है!!

हाँ हो रहा है
मुझे तुमसे इश्क़!!"

Sakshi Sharma

Ms. Sakshi Sharma hails from Aligarh, U.P. She like to decorate her words and emotions on paper and has participated in various anthologies as co-author. She is biotechnologist and researcher by profession with more than 2 years of experience. Additionally, she is national kathak dancer. She wants to be unique! to stand out amongst the people and like to learn new things. She believes in delivering smiles on the faces.

आसान है क्या,

आसान है क्या,
हंसी में यूँही गम को छुपा लेना,
तड़पती रूह को झूठा दिलासा देना,
बारिश की बूंदों से अश्क़ों को भिगा लेना,
आसान है क्या,
अधूरी यादों को सजा लेना,
डूबती कश्ती को बचा लेना,
बिखरती जुल्फ़ों को संवार लेना,
आसान है क्या,
हर ज़रर पे मरहम का लेप करना,
चहरे पे तबस्सुम का निखार करना,
नाइत्तेफाकी में भी अपनी बात रखना,
आसान है क्या,
नाखुशी में भी मुस्कुराके बात करना,
ज़िंदा रहके भी नाबूद-ऐ-जिस्म रहना,
नुमाइश-ऐ-ज़िल्लत में भी मौन रहना,
आसान है क्या,
बिखरती राहों में सँवरके चलना,
यह आसान तो नहीं, नज़्म में हर गम को पढ़ना,
आसान है क्या, सिर्फ लिखके दर्द को बयां करना,
आसान है क्या,

अफ़साना

अज़ीज़ इतने हो तुम इस दिल के,
अफ़साना पढ़ती हूँ सांझ सवेरे...
आराइश भी बुझ गयी अब तो दिल की,
दरमियान रहा ना जब कुछ तेरे और मेरे,
इत्तिहाम तो ना हमारा था और ना तुम्हारा,
इब्तिला मिली हमें तो किस्मत से...
इश्तियाक़ तो ये है, की बसा लें तुमको मन में,
पर इल्म नहीं था इतना कि बहेंगे यूँ अश्क़ों में,
कायल हम तो हैं तुम्हारे, क़ज़ा मिले कभी क़ाज़ी से...
अज़ीज़ इतने हो तुम इस दिल के,
अफ़साना पढ़ती हूँ सांझ सवेरे...

Debesh Prusty

Debesh lays his foundation for his books from graduation time. He loves to write microtales from his young age. For the first time he stepped in to spotlight. Growing up with several failures but he never lose hope. We hope you will love to read his writings.

Love is the secret of happiness

Everyone wants to be happy in this world. But there are only a few people who are happy. Somepeople believe that wealth gives happiness.Thats why they trying to acquire it more and more. But in reality it just give us happiness which exists for a certain period of time. Money just give us basic materialistic comforts which makes us happy for temporary time , it can't give the emotional and spiritual satisfaction.

While some of others believe that gaining power will give happiness. But even such powers cann't give you happiness for lifetime . In present age,many people strive for happiness in sex, fashion, drinks and drugs. These things may help people to forget their worries for a limited period of time but not forever. Most of them are harmful rather than helpful.

Only a few know the secret of true happiness. It is the love that makes man's life meaningful ful.

Love is not only meant for bf/ gf but also between parents children, brother and sister, teacher and student. Selfless love carries your life to that height where you canfind out the true meaning of peaceful and blissful life.

कैसे देखूँ उन्हे इस बूढ़ापे में

कैसे देखूँ उन्हे इस बूढ़ापे में
दर्द होता है सिने में:
क्यूं बोझ लगता है वो कंधे
जिन पर चढ़ कर हुम दुनिया देखा करते थे
निस्वार्थ प्यार किया उन्होने
अपनी ज़रूरत को भुलाया उन्होने।
उनके जैसा प्यार हमे कौन करेगा
जो भी करेगा वो किमत मांगगेगा
मैं रोया भी करता हुँ परदेस में
याद करके मा का प्यार
मा ने दिल की हर एक बात समझी
बिना चिट्टी बिना तार।
जितना भू लिखूं उनके लिये कम है
वो है इस लिये हम हम है
कैसे देखूँ उन्हे इस बूढ़ापे में
दर्द होता है सिने में
रब को माँगू दुआ में उमर देदो उनको मेरे सारे।।

Gautam Kushwah

A calm and composed individual with a flamboyant side.
Loves writing, the asphalt and the adventures it brings.
Sometimes hedonistic, a little too much for his own good.

Will you stay?

I enter, stumbling, slurring, running into things
Professing my love, maybe embarrassing you
With my imprudent ways, onto the floor i lay
Asking you
Will you stay?

For months I pursued us,
Tears had washed all my sins away
Debauchery stayed, sincerity waved
From the edge as you watched
The road less travelled by was yawing on the way
Will you stay?

Promises broken, and upheld
Different lives led
A glass of wine, raillery
Accompanied with scotch
Unburnt cigarettes in the ashtray
Will you Stay?

Love is all we need?
We need something more strong
No point pointing fingers
In the end we are all wrong
Will you work with me on this
In the midnight with me
Will you lay
Will you stay?

Friends or so they call themselves
Love or so it wants to be called
I don't know what we share
I don't know if we share anything at all

The bard and the Rogue

The bard walked on the cobbled street
Singing stories of his lost love,
Of empires and the greats that lived once.
Of courage and all things cliche
The rogue stood there in the crowd,
Her hand constantly on the dagger,
Which has protected her before
From all the evil she projected on the world

The stories had something about them,
The rogue couldn't resist their charm,
The bard couldn't resist her's,
The Rogue being a rogue couldn't be trusted
But like all the bards before and all the bards that were to
come
Poetic sense prevailed, poetic justice not so much
The bard sings no more
The Rogue being a rogue couldn't be trusted

Vaibhava Suri

Vaibhava Suri is a compassionate poet, writer & novelist, who loves to pen down his emotions & thoughts in such a way, which may arise tears in the eyes of the readers. He is the one who exhibits the guts in penning down the weaknesses of the society, highlighting the social taboos prevailing in the country

My Love

Believe it or not
You are my love
The day we don't have a conversation
It is not possible for me to sleep all night

Now your heart has become my treasure
You are my love, you are my love
Can't sleep all night, only you are the remembrance
But now we will meet after the lockdown would end

For me you are like a Manjha tied to my kite
Since when we are together, I m carefree

If love is a drug, you are its drug
Come, my honey, come with me
I respect your duty
Uff... your words, Uff... your beauty

You are the most unique companion
You are my charioteer more than love
Neither mind is under control nor my heart
Because you are the only princess of this heart

Heart wants me to just get lost in your style
I don't wanna listen to any, just wanna come to you

When I cried, you gave cured the wounds of my heart
When I was not in good state, you smiled and filled the emotion of happiness
Then became a necessary companion of my success
You became a charioteer when I got upset...

Krishna Motwani

Krishna Motwani is a Student currently.
She use to pen down her feelings.
She is a moody girl.
She started writing in the month of june,2020.
She writes in her free time.
She writes some motivational quotes or poetries too and practices artworks also.
She lives her life like a bird
As bird flies freely and enjoys life like that she also lives her life freely and enjoy fullest.
For motivating and inspiring poems and quotes, you can check her on instagram : @ unique__blog_

<u>रो रहा है उसका दिल!</u>

थक गया है उसका दिल तुम्हें याद करते करते,
मरने पे पड़ी है आज वो तुम्हें सोचते सोचते।

तुम्हारे बिना उसका दिल लगता नहीं कहीं,
कुछ भी उसे लगता नहीं सही।

पहले तुम्हारे कहने पर थोड़ा खा लेती थी,
वह तुमसे बहुत प्यार करती है और करती थी।

कब तो तुम आ जाओ,
यूँ तो उसे ना सताओ।

तुमने किसी और से प्यार किया,
यह सुनकर तो उसने सब कुछ त्याग दिया।

तुम्हारे बिना है वो अदूरी अब भी,
बहुत करती है तुमसे प्यार आज भी।

Jayashree Sahoo

Jayashree Sahoo is habitant of ODISHA .
Nowadays She is member of many writing communities and earned a alots of certificates through her writings .
She is Co.author of 160+ anthologies .Also She is Compiler of many anthologies in Hindi ,English and Odia languages .
According to her,if you dont express your inner feelings towards someone,then just write those on a paper and making yourself happy for without reason .
Insta id -@mixing_of_emotions
Email.id- jayashreesahoo665@gmail.com

Love you more

You are mine forever,
I ll wait for u forever,
Just say me in loyalty ,
Do u love me in reality, ?
Somewhere I found many fake ,
So I dont want to do any mistake ,
If your love is true and pure ,
Dont proof it by doing better,
Just love me from your hearty inner,
It ll give me more and more pleasure,
You know I kept some surprises,
But I dont give you in easy case,
You have to be loyal and my halfbetter,
Then I ll trust you more than me in future,
I know attraction is so easy for falling in love,
But I think , somewhere hard trust with dedication is best
more than love ,
So how much u attractive in outside ,that doesn't matter ,
Your sincierity and loyalty always matter forever ,
I wish I do love you daily in perfect pure ,
So atlast just wanna tell you "I love you more "

Oh dear

Wherever I see it
"It simply came to our notice
then I love you
I couldn't think of myself without you
My creation is only for you I love you ,
 I want to be with you
forever every moment..
 I smile because of I love you
 You are still far from me
 But your heart is always with me
 I lost my sleep for you
I see your dream is empty I love you ..

Pratham Mittal

He is very Positive, kind, helpful, friendly and happy soul. His passion is painting and writing. He has won many competitions, published in many books, participated in International Writing Competitions.

Love and Friendship

Love is just like the wild rose-briar,
Friendship just like the holly-tree—
The holly is dark when the rose-briar blooms
But which can bloom most constantly?

The wild rose-briar is nice in spring,
Its summer blossoms scent the air;
Yet wait till winter comes again
And who will call the wild-briar fair?

Then scorn the silly rose-wreath now
And deck thee with the holly's sheen,
That when December blights thy brow
He still may leave thy garland green.

The Importance Of A Sister

A sister is someone who loves you from the guts .
No matter what proportion you argue, you can't be drawn apart.
She may be a joy that can't be removed .
Once she enters your life, she is there to remain .
A friend who helps you thru difficult times,
Her comforting words are worth far more than dimes.
A Life partner who fills your life with laughs and smiles,
These memories last for miles and miles.
When she is by your side, the planet is crammed with life.
When she isn't around, your days are filled with strife.
A sister may be a blessing who fills your heart amorously .
She flies with you in life with the sweetness of a dove.
A companion to whom you'll express your feelings,
She doesn't allow you to get bored at family dealings.
Whether you're having your ups or downs,
She always helps you with a smile whenever you needs.
With a sister, you can't have a grudge.
She is as sweet as chocolate.
Having a sister isn't just a trend.

Arju Mali

She is a student of Bachelor of Arts. She writes with lots of love, emotions and truthfulness. Her writings mostly portray courage and extend motivation. She is also the co- author of many Anthologies. Writing is her passion.*
Instagram: @Arju mali25

Is Pyaar ko Kya Naam du....

Ek ladka tha or Ek ladki Thi do no ki life story kuch Esi thi
Dono ka Saath Accha tha
Dono ka Pyaar Saccha tha
Dono ka Future Secure tha
Dono Ek dujee Ko Smjte the
Dono Ek Dusre ko Pura krte the
Har Pal Har lamha bss
Dono ko Ek Duje ka Saath chaiye tha..

Ek duje ko Sab batana unka vishvas tha
Ek Duje ko Special Fill Krana Pyar tha
Inke Bich ladaiyaa bhi bhut hoti Thi
Qki dono ki Choice thodi Alg thi
Par dono ek Duje ki Best choice the...

Is Pyaare Se Riste me ek ladki ka aana bhi Ek modd tha jo har
kahani me aata hai or us kahani ko Pura hone se rokta he us
Ladki ki soch us ladke se milti Thi
Dono ki Jada banne lagi
Dono ki Baate bdne lagi
Ladke ko Ladki Pasand aane lagi
Yeh Pasand Sirf Tym pass tha
Yeh Us ladki ko Bataya tha un dono ke bich me esa modd bhi
aana tha
Kehna yeah tha ki Ese Dhoka nhi keh Sakte
Haa shi he Qki ladki ko Sab pehle Se hi Pta tha
Isse keh skte hai tho Sirf yeh

"Mohhabat ke Bich koii   Teesra"
Its complicated.....

Flairs and Glairs, a platform by a student for the students. We are esteemed youth struggling to carve out our path for our future and we follow a basic mindset Since everyone is not born with all-round skills. Joining hands with people who are born to execute it with perfection is the best way to evolve. Self-Evolution is the need of the hour but, evolving as a community is what we strive for. The initiative as kickstarted by, Founder- Mr. Shubham Shah with the motive to utilize the skillset and talent of writing has now a team of 10+ people who are actively participating into newer forms of learning and discovering talents among youngsters. We Provide platform and services like Publishing opportunities, Open mics, Workshops, Hands-on training. Operating with Brand Name of Flairs and Glairs (Publication House), we offer the chance of elevating a passionate writer to an esteemed author With Brand name Teekhe Zasbaaat. We bring to you an opportunity to get accustomed with the Public Speaking and Presenting of Thoughts along with regular challenges to brush up your inking spirit. The newest initiative to extend our services we introduced in a new writing Platform- The Glittering Fables and Ink Over Tears.

We Choose to Fly Like A Falcon than to be

a Leg Pulling Crab.

To Know More: Infoline – 7781900870
Mail Us At-
flairsandglairs@gmail.com / info@flairsandglairs.in
Or Visit is at
www.flairsandglairs.com / www.flairsandglairs.in
Social Handles- @flairsandglairs @teekhezasbaaat

www.ingramcontent.com/pod-product-compliance
Lightning Source LLC
LaVergne TN
LVHW010017200726
843495LV00015B/1811